The Curse

The Curse

CONFRONTING

THE LAST

UNMENTIONABLE

TABOO:

MENSTRUATION

KAREN HOUPPERT

Farrar, Straus and Giroux

NEW YORK

Farrar, Straus and Giroux
19 Union Square West, New York 10003

Copyright © 1999 by Karen Houppert
All rights reserved
Distributed in Canada by Douglas & McIntyre Ltd.
Printed in the United States of America
Designed by Abby Kagan
First edition, 1999

Library of Congress Cataloging-in-Publication Data
Houppert, Karen, 1956–
    The curse : confronting the last unmentionable taboo: menstruation
    / Karen Houppert. — 1st ed.
        p.   cm.
    ISBN 0-374-27366-9 (alk. paper)
        1. Menstruation—Social aspects.   2. Menstruation—Public opinion.
    I. Title.
    GN484.38.H68   1999
    612.6'62—dc21   98-45364

See pages 257–258 for Permissions

FOR KIA